THE BIG COMFY COUCH™

It's Taking Too Long!

Written by **Cheryl Wagner**

Illustrated by **Richard Kolding**

TIME LIFE Kids.

ALEXANDRIA, VIRGINIA

One day Molly the doll had a big idea. "Oh, you want to go fishing, Molly," said Loonette. "All right. The Big Comfy Couch can be our boat. We can make our own fishing poles. It will be fun!"

Loonette knew that fishing was Molly's favorite thing to do. Molly loved to be in the Big Comfy boat with her best clown friend. Today she might catch a whale! Or maybe even a goldfish. Loonette wanted to catch a clownfish.

Of course, it is hard for little clowns to sit still for long, even in a Big Comfy boat. Soon Loonette felt wiggly. Then she felt squiggly. And there was still no clownfish on her special hook. "Picklejuice!" muttered Loonette.

Loonette wiggled and squiggled.

Molly giggled.

"It isn't funny, Molly!"
said the little clown.

"I can't wait all day to catch a fish.
It's taking too long!"

Then Loonette had a big idea. Maybe there was a postcard or package in her mailbox. That would be more fun than boring old fishing. Loonette decided to go outside and check.

Empty! "Double picklejuice!" Loonette exclaimed.

Major Bedhead, the clown who brought the mail, hadn't even been there yet. Loonette sat down to wait for him.

She waited. And waited. And waited some more. "I can't wait all day for a postcard! It's taking too long!"

Just then, Loonette smelled something yummy—borscht brownies, her favorite. Granny Garbanzo had just taken some out of the oven.

"Can I please have a brownie, Granny?" Loonette asked, using her best manners.

"Not just yet, Loonette," Granny said. "They're too hot to eat."

Loonette had to wait for them to cool.

Loonette waited. And waited. And waited some more.
It was taking FOREVER for those brownies to cool.

Loonette felt as if she were going to explode. "I can't wait all day for my brownie! It's taking too long!" she complained.

Granny understood Loonette's problem. "I think a little clown needs to learn a little patience," she said. "Patience means you have to wait, and that's not easy—even for big clowns like me."

So Granny showed Loonette her special patience trick. "When you have to wait . . . just put your finger on your nose and count to eight."

Loonette tried it. "One, two, three, four, five, six, seven, eight!" It was fun!

Major Bedhead
arrived just in
time for a nice,
warm borscht
brownie with
Granny and
Loonette. Before
he had his snack,
he stuck his
hand into his
mailbag.

"There's
something here
for you, Loonette,"
he told her.

He dug deeper. And deeper. And deeper still.

Loonette waited. And waited. And waited some more. But she was very patient. Patience means you have to wait.

Finally Major Bedhead pulled a postcard from his mailbag and handed it to Loonette. She was so happy she had waited.

Loonette was excited to show Molly her new special trick. It was fun! Now fishing on the Big Comfy boat was more fun too, because Loonette knew how to be patient.

While the two best friends waited to catch a whale—or even a goldfish—Loonette sang Molly a little song she made up about patience.

"Patience means you have to wait
Touch your nose and count to eight
One, two, three, four, five, six, seven . . ."

Sing to the tune of "Mary Had a Little Lamb"

Patience means you have to wait
Have to wait
Have to wait
When you know you have to wait
There's something you can do.

Touch your nose and count to eight
Count to eight
Count to eight
Even though you hate to wait
This trick will work for you.

Every time it's hard to wait,
Dad or Mom's running late,
Touch your nose and count to eight
Don't sit around and stew!

One, two-three-four five, six, seven
Five, six, seven
Five, six, seven
One, two-three-four five, six, seven—
EIGHT, now we are through!